O·l·i·v·e
marshmallow

By Katie Saunders

little bee books

This is Archie.

Archie is a little boy who lives in a BIG house.
Archie loves lots of things, like planes, robots, and football.

And Archie loves his mom and dad.

But lately, there's something a bit different about Mom...

"What's going on?" Archie wonders.
"Mommy looks . . . BIGGER."

Mommy's office is suddenly different, too.
"Everything is **pink**!" Archie says.

Princess
Sleeping

"Why is my house full of **fluffy**, **frilly**, very pink things?"

Mommy shows Archie a strange picture.

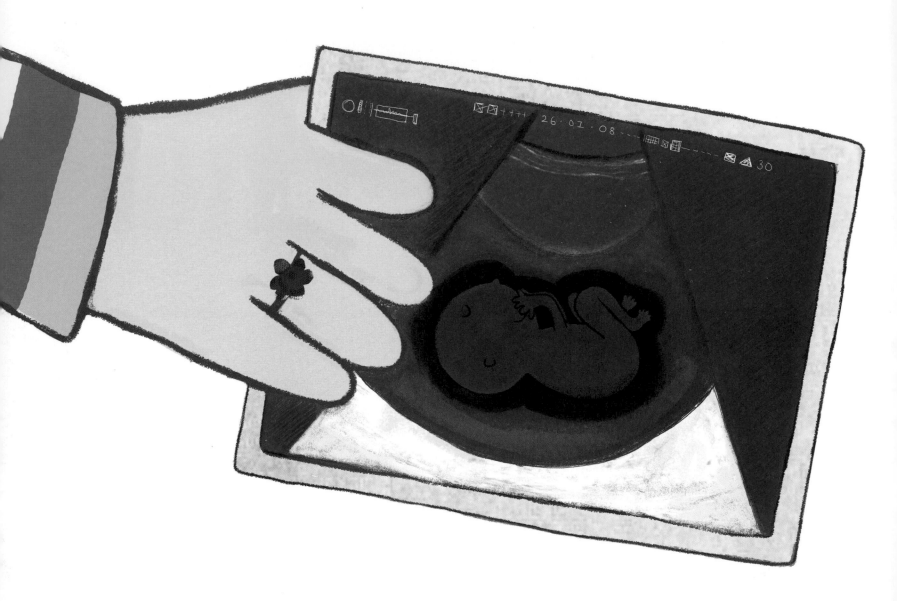

"This is your baby sister growing in Mommy's tummy," she says.

Archie thinks it looks a bit like an alien.

Archie isn't sure that he wants a baby sister.
He likes cars, trains, and playing ninjas.

He is ABSOLUTELY sure that he doesn't like fluffy, frilly, very **pink** things.

One night, Mommy goes to the hospital for a sleepover.
She takes a little bag and her toothbrush,
and she says she won't be gone for long.

She also tells Archie she will bring him back a surprise.
Archie doesn't want Mommy to go anywhere.

But he is really looking forward to a surprise.

When Mommy comes home, she is carrying a fluffy, frilly, very **pink** bundle.
"This is Olive," says Mommy.

Archie laughs.

"She looks just like a
marshmallow!"

"Congratulations, Archie!" says Mommy. "You are a big brother." Mom gives Archie a special toy. "This is from Olive."

Being a big brother might be nice after all...
even if it means playing with fluffy, frilly, very pink things.

Soon, life with Olive Marshmallow...

became so much

FUN!

Now there are twice as many toys!

And Archie always has someone to play with.

"Little sisters are actually really great. Even if sometimes they do look like fluffy pink **marshmallows!**"

"I'm glad you came to live with us, Olive!"

Olive doesn't have much to say yet.
But she does give Archie a big, amazing smile.

Then one day, Archie and Olive
    notice something different about Mom....

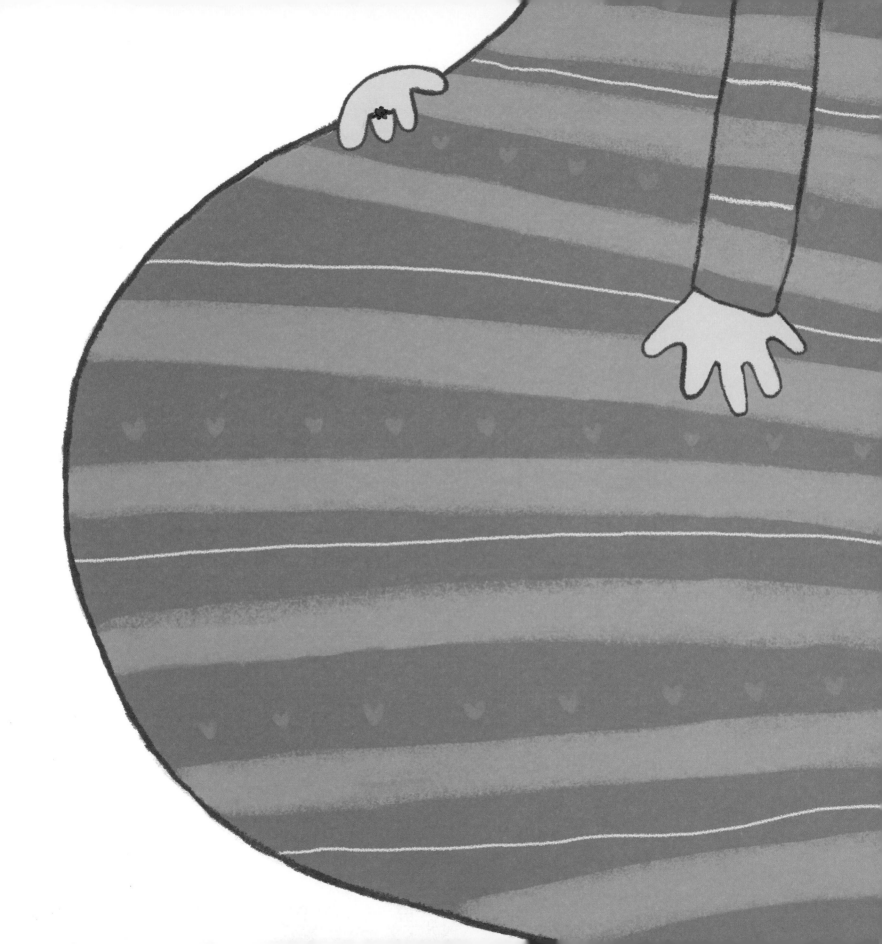

For Archie Gray and Olive Honey
love Mommy xxxx

and William
for help with the title

little bee books
An imprint of Bonnier Publishing Group
853 Broadway, New York, New York 10003
Text and illustration copyright © 2014 by Katie Saunders.
First published in Australia by The Five Mile Press.
This little bee books edition, 2015.
All rights reserved, including the right of reproduction in whole
or in part in any form. LITTLE BEE BOOKS is a trademark of
Bonnier Publishing Group, and associated colophon is a trademark
of Bonnier Publishing Group.
Manufactured in China 1014 HH
First Edition 2 4 6 8 10 9 7 5 3 1
Library of Congress Control Number: 2014943629
ISBN 978-1-4998-0019-7

www.littlebeebooks.com
www.bonnierpublishing.com